# Little Mouse & Elephant

*A TALE FROM TURKEY*

RETOLD BY
## Jane Yolen

ILLUSTRATED BY
## John Segal

Simon & Schuster Books for Young Readers

AUTHOR'S NOTE

This Turkish story has links with Arabic and Persian tales about
similar numbskulls. Such silly stories can be found in the Turkish
"jestbooks," books made up of humorous jokes, anecdotes, and tales.

SIMON & SCHUSTER BOOKS FOR YOUNG READERS
An imprint of Simon & Schuster Children's Publishing Division
1230 Avenue of the Americas, New York, New York 10020
Text copyright © 1996 by Jane Yolen. Illustrations copyright © 1996 by John Segal.
All rights reserved including the right of reproduction in whole or in part in any form.
SIMON & SCHUSTER BOOKS FOR YOUNG READERS is a trademark of Simon & Schuster.
Book design by Paul Zakris. The text for this book is set in 18-point Venetian.
The illustrations are rendered in watercolor.
Manufactured in the United Sates of America
First Edition
10 9 8 7 6 5 4 3 2 1

Library of Congress Cataloging-in-Publication Data
Yolen, Jane.
Little Mouse and Elephant : a tale from Turkey / retold by Jane Yolen; illustrated by John Segal.
p.    cm.
Summary: Boastful Little Mouse sets out to show that he is stronger than anyone
in the forest, even Elephant, and nothing that happens can change his opinion.
ISBN 0-689-80493-8
[1. Folklore—Turkey. 2. Mice—Folklore. 3. Elephants—Folklore.] I. Segal, John, ill. II. Title.
PZ8.1.Y815Li    1996    398.2'09561—dc20    [E]    94-30731

*For Maddison Jane Piatt,*
*a small book for small hands*
—J. Y.

*To Emily, with love*
—J. S.

There was once a mouse, a little mouse, whose pride was much greater than his sense.

"I am the strongest animal around," he announced to anyone who would listen.

His grandfather cautioned him. "Your body is little, but your mouth is large, child, much larger than your brain. If you are not careful, Elephant will hear you."

"Elephant!" laughed Little Mouse, for he had never seen him. "Who is he that I should care?"

"He is the master of the forest," said Grandfather.

"He cannot be," said Little Mouse, puffing up his chest. "*I* am."

Grandfather smiled behind his paw. "Some must learn by seeing for themselves," he said. "Off you go."

"Off I go indeed," said Little Mouse. "I shall teach this Elephant a lesson or two."

He walked away without looking back and soon came to a green creature sunning itself on a rock.

"Hey, you lazybones," called out Little Mouse, "are you this Elephant my grandfather talks of?"

"Oh, no," hissed the green creature carefully. "I am only Lizard."

"Lucky for you," said Little Mouse. "If you had been Elephant, I would have broken you to bits."

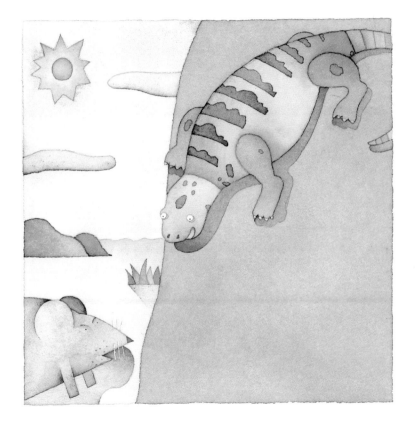

Lizard had seen Elephant, so he laughed a hissy little laugh. When Little Mouse heard that, he grew furious and stamped his paw.

Now it happened that at that very moment there was a loud clap of thunder in the east. Lizard, who liked sun and not rain, scuttled under a bush.

Little Mouse puffed out his chest.

"Lizard knows who is master here," he said, and walked on.

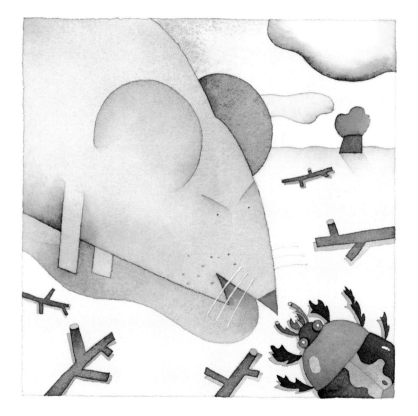

Soon he came to a shiny blue creature creeping carefully over twigs.

"Hey, you slowpoke," called out Little Mouse, "are you this Elephant I have heard so much about?"

"Oh, no," said the shiny blue creature in a crackly voice. "I am only Beetle."

"Lucky for you," said Little Mouse. "If you had been Elephant, I would have broken you to bits."

Beetle, who had seen Elephant, shrugged his shoulders, which made his shell hump up a bit. At that exact moment there came a flash of lightning in the west. Worried about storms, Beetle scuttered away.

If anything, that puffed up Little Mouse more than before. "Beetle knows who is master here," he said, and walked on.

At a bend in the road he saw a rather large brown creature sitting in the dirt.

"Hey, you rear-in-the-dust," called out Little Mouse, "are you this Elephant everyone speaks of?"

"Elephant? Not I," said the brown creature. "I am only Dog." He smiled eagerly and wagged his not inconsiderable tail back and forth, stirring the dirt.

"Oh you may smile," said Little Mouse, "but had you been Elephant, I would have broken you to bits."

Now Dog had seen Elephant, and he was about to answer Little Mouse back when there was a sudden loud whistle. Dog stood at once. "That is master," he said.

Little Mouse replied angrily, "I am the only master here."

But Dog had already run off without a backward glance. Little Mouse was so furious, he didn't watch the path as he walked, and he bumped right into a mountain.

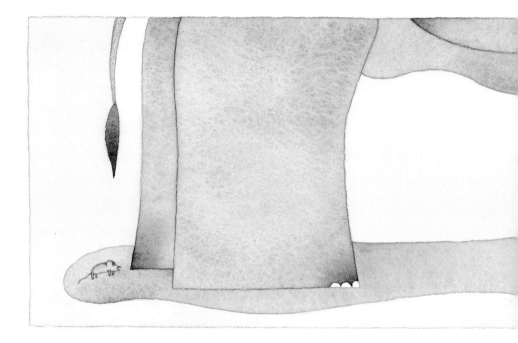

Only it was not exactly a mountain, but
an enormous gray creature with four legs as

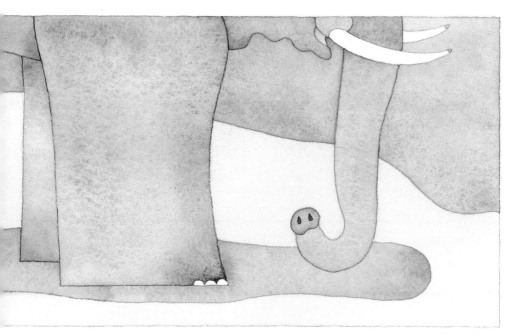

large and solid as oak trunks. It had two tails,
a large one in front and a smaller one behind.

"Hey, you gray mountain," called out Little Mouse, "are you Elephant?"

The gray creature heard the voice but could not see who was speaking. He looked from tree to rock to riverbank trying to find the speaker. At last he looked right down by his left back leg, and there was a very small dot with a very large voice.

"Move out of my way!" called out Little Mouse.

The gray creature did not move.

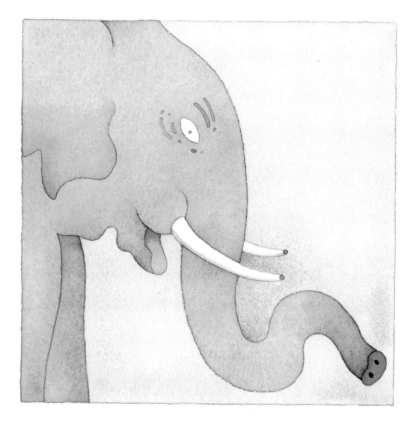

"And who do you think you are not to move?" asked Little Mouse.

"Elephant," said Elephant. But his voice was funny, as if he had a stuffy nose.

"Ah—Elephant!" said Little Mouse. "Just the one I have been seeking. Did you know that I am master of the forest? Lizard and Beetle and Dog"—he was not *quite* sure about Dog—"all agree. Move along or I shall break you to bits."

Elephant cast a calculating eye at the talking speck, then aimed his trunk at it.

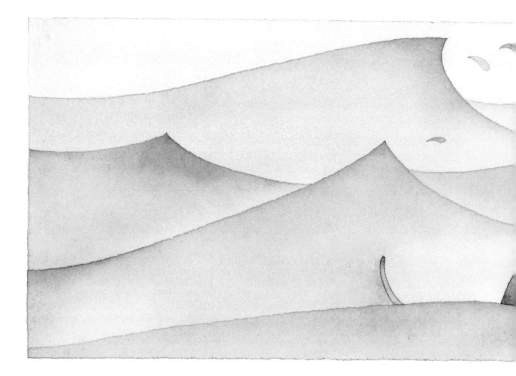

All the water he had sucked up for his bath

gushed forth in one great and terrible *whooooosh*.

Little Mouse went head over tail, head over tail, and fetched up against a tree. When he came to his senses at last, Elephant was gone.

"What a storm!" said Little Mouse. "And it's mighty lucky for Elephant it came when it did. Otherwise I would have broken him to bits."

He turned and went back home, his chest all puffed out, singing a song that went like this:

*Lizard knows it, knows it, knows it,*
*Beetle shows it, shows it, shows it,*
*Dog admits it, 'mits it, 'mits it,*
*Elephant ran away.*

When he reached home, he told Grand-father and the other mice all about his great adventure. And no one could get him to change a word.

If Elephant has not come by since to dispute it, Little Mouse is still telling that same tale, which is how I first heard it. And now you have heard it from me.